To Adam, our sweetheart,
with love, hugs and kisses from
Mum, Dad, Harry, Robbie and Molly.

Adam is an angel and lives on a cloud
and makes his Mummy and Daddy so proud.
With long golden hair you just could not miss,
he always has time for a hug and a kiss.
The message he sends from his cloud every day,
is to spend more time with each other and play.
The most important thing in life is this,
show your love for your family with a hug and a kiss.

Written by Benji Bennett.
benji@adamsprintingpress.ie

Illustrations by Roxanne Burchartz of Cartoon Saloon.
www.cartoonsaloon.ie

Designed by Bold.
www.reallybold.com

Printed by Watermans Printers
www.watermansprinters.ie
ISBN 978-1-906818-03-6

Published by

Adam's Printing Press is dedicated to spreading Adam's message of the importance of love, laughter and play within the family
and will make a donation from the proceeds of all books published under its imprint to children's charities.

Adam's Printing Press
PO Box 11379, Blackrock, Co. Dublin, Ireland
Email: info@adamsprintingpress.ie
Web: www.adamsprintingpress.ie
Tel: +353 1 2833620

A donation of 2% of the recommended retail price of this book will go to

Founded by Paul Newman in 1994, Barretstown exists to improve the quality of life of children with serious illness
by providing life changing programmes of therapeutic recreation which aim to rebuild their confidence, trust and self esteem.
Hospitals take care of the physical effect of serious illness; Barretstown helps to heal the emotional scars.

It's time to sleep but before you go, there is

I love you much more than the deepest blue sea

To dress up as pirates and find us some treasure

something I really want you to know.

I love it so much when you swim beside me

would be something we would always remember forever.

Who is Adam? He is so scary.
He has a patch on his eye and a beard that's so hairy.

At the end of one arm for a hand is a hook,
That was given to him by a crookedly crook.

The hat on his head is all battered and torn,
It's been stuck to his head since the day he was born.

Under his hat are his gold curly locks,
And through a hole in his boot see the holes in his socks.

With a skull and crossbones on his belt for a buckle,
He wears a big gold ring right up to his knuckle.

When he smiles a big smile and shows his golden tooth
That's how you know when he's telling the truth.

In a secret pocket hidden under his vest,
He keeps a key safe for his treasure chest.

So full of smiles with hilarious wit,
Have you guessed that Adam is a friendly....

...Pirate!

"Come on!" said Adam to the girls and boys,
"Let's take to the seas and find us some toys."
With a hop and a skip they jumped on to their ship,
Hoisted the sails and set off on their trip.
As Fluff filled the sails when he started to blow,
The crew shouted to Adam saying, "Where will we go?"
"We'll follow the stars to a tropical land,"
Said Adam, as he opened the map in his hand.
He smiled his big smile and showed his golden tooth,
So all the crew knew he was telling the truth.

"Aye, Aye, Captain Adam, we'll take your advice,"
Said the crew, who thought Adam was really quite nice.
They followed the stars for a day and a night
And could not believe Captain Adam was right.

"Land Ho!" shouted Molly, high up in the mast,
"We've found the Island with treasure at last."
"Well done, Captain Adam," cheered the whole pirate crew
Then they all rowed to shore in a boat made for two.

The pirates all cheered when they hit dry land,
And everyone searched for the X in the sand.
Robbie is Adam's best boy in the crew,
"Look!" he said, "Adam, I found this for you."
"Well shiver me timbers," Adam said, with a grin,
"You found the X in the sand let the digging begin."

Pirate Jack started digging with his bucket and spade,
While Adam and Harry played snap in the shade.
"Thump, thump," went the spade on the big treasure chest,
They found it at last then sat down for a rest.

Adam jumped up, and said, "Lad's you're the best,"
Then pulled out the key of the chest from his vest.
In went the key and clunk went the lock,
As he wiggled his toe through the hole in his sock.

The chest opened up and eyes opened wide,
Then Adam gave Robbie a grin full of pride.
"This is the best treasure we've ever found,"
Said Robbie, to Adam as the lock hit the ground.

When the lid of the treasure chest opened up wide,
Robbie tipped on his toes for the first peek inside.
"This is supreme," he said with a scream,
"There are so many toys this must be a dream."

He could not believe all the things that he saw,
Stickers and games and a drink with a straw,
Dressing up costumes and colouring pens,
And a bat and a ball to play with his friends.

"Well blow me down" said Adam,
"it's time for some grub,
But before we eat let's play golf with this club.
First prize is a sausage wrapped up in a bun,
For the pirate who scores us
the first hole-in-one."

With a chip and a putt
the ball started to roll,
It hit the flag pole
and fell into the hole.
"Well done! You won
a sausage and bun,"
Said Adam to Robbie,
for his hole-in-one.

The whole pirate crew had lunch and a drink,
Till Adam lifted his patch and gave Robbie a wink.
"Time for more fun and a big football match,"
Said Adam to Robbie, as he pulled down his patch.
The crew passed to each other with brilliant control,
Then passed it to Robbie who scored a great goal.
"Goooooal!" shouted Robbie, as he jumped up and down,
Then ran around the chest like a big circus clown.

Adam looked at the sun as it started to set,
At the end of a day he would never forget.
"Time to finish our big treasure hunt,"
Adam declared, with a bit of a grunt.
They buried the chest and went back to the ship,
And before they set sail walked the plank for a dip.
They hoisted the anchor and pulled back the oars,
Then waved goodbye to the treasure-filled shores.

With his big shiny tooth and his map in his hand,
Adam was happy with the day that he planned.
He plotted a course through the magical seas,
Then the sails of the ship filled up in a breeze.
He climbed down below to his big pirate's bed,
And dropped off to sleep with his hat on his head.

It's time to sleep my favourite pirate
From your nose to your toes I love you every bit
I love you much more than all the world's treasure
Sweet dreams, my love, I'll love you forever.